Treasured T...

Goldilocks
and the
Three Bears

p

Once upon a time, deep in a dark green forest, there lived a family of bears. There was great big Daddy Bear. There was middle-sized Mummy Bear. And there was little Baby Bear.

One sunny morning, the bears were up early, hungry for their breakfast. Daddy Bear cooked three bowls of porridge. He made it with lots of golden, runny honey, just the way bears like it. "Breakfast is ready!" called Daddy Bear.

But when he poured it into the bowls, it was far too hot to eat!

"We'll just have to let our porridge cool down for a while before we eat it," said Mummy Bear.

"But I'm hungry!" wailed Baby Bear.

"I know, let's go for a walk in the forest while we wait," suggested Mummy Bear. "Get the basket, Baby Bear. We can gather some wild berries as we go."

So, leaving the steaming bowls of porridge on the table, the three bears went out into the forest. The last one out was little Baby Bear, and he forgot to close the front door behind him.

The sun was shining brightly through the trees that morning and someone else was walking in the forest. It was a little girl called Goldilocks, who had long, curly golden hair and the cutest nose you ever did see.

Goldilocks was skipping happily through the forest when suddenly she smelt something yummy and delicious – whatever could it be?

She followed the smell until she came to the three bears' cottage. It seemed to be coming from inside. The door was open, so she peeped in and saw three bowls of porridge on the table.

Goldilocks just couldn't resist the lovely sweet smell. So, even though she knew she wasn't ever supposed to go into anyone's house without first being invited, she tiptoed inside.

First, she tasted the porridge in Daddy Bear's great big bowl. "Ouch!" she said. "This porridge is *far* too hot!" So she tried the porridge in Mummy Bear's middle-sized bowl. "Yuck!" said Goldilocks. "This porridge is *far* too sweet!" Finally, she tried the porridge in Baby Bear's tiny little bowl. "Yummy!" she said, licking her lips. "This porridge is *just right*!" So Goldilocks ate it *all* up – every last drop!

Goldilocks was so full up after eating Baby Bear's porridge that she decided she must sit down. First, she tried sitting in Daddy Bear's great big chair. "Oh, dear!" she said. "This chair is *far* too hard!" So she tried Mummy Bear's middle-sized chair. "Oh, no!" said Goldilocks. "This chair is *far* too soft!" Finally, Goldilocks tried Baby Bear's tiny little chair. "Hurray!" she cried. "This chair is *just right*!" So she stretched out and made herself very comfortable.

But Baby Bear's chair wasn't *just right*! It was *far* too small and, as Goldilocks settled down, it broke into lots of little pieces!

Goldilocks picked herself up off the floor and brushed down her dress. Trying out all of those chairs had made her *very* tired. She looked around the cottage for a place to lie down and soon found the three bears' bedroom.

First, Goldilocks tried Daddy Bear's great big bed. "Oh, this won't do!" she said. "This bed is *far* too hard!" So she tried Mummy Bear's middle-sized bed. "Oh, bother!" said Goldilocks. "This bed is *far* too soft!" Finally, she tried Baby Bear's tiny little bed. "Yippee!" she cried. "This bed is *just right*!" So Goldilocks climbed in, pulled the blanket up to her chin and fell fast, fast asleep.

Not long after, the three bears came home from their walk, ready for their yummy porridge. But as soon as they entered their little cottage, they knew something wasn't quite right.

"Someone's been eating my porridge!" said Daddy Bear, when he looked at his great big bowl.

"Someone's been eating my porridge!" said Mummy Bear, looking at her middle-sized bowl.

"Someone's been eating *my* porridge," cried Baby Bear, looking sadly at his tiny little bowl. "And they've eaten it *all up*!"

Then Daddy Bear noticed that his chair had been moved. "Look, Mummy Bear! Someone's been sitting in my chair!" he said in his deep, gruff voice.

"Look, Daddy Bear! Someone's been sitting in my chair," said Mummy Bear, as she straightened the cushions on it.

"Someone's been sitting in *my* chair, too," cried Baby Bear. "And look! They've broken it all to pieces!" They all stared at the bits of broken chair. Then Baby Bear burst into tears.

Suddenly, the three bears heard the tiniest of noises. Was it a creak? Was it a groan? No, it was a snore, and it was coming from their bedroom. They crept up the stairs very, very quietly, to see what was making the noise…

"Someone's been sleeping in my bed!" cried Daddy Bear.

"Someone's been sleeping in my bed," said Mummy Bear.

"Someone's been sleeping in *my* bed!" cried Baby Bear. "And she's still there!"

All this noise woke Goldilocks up with a start.

When she saw the three bears standing over her, Goldilocks was very scared. "Oh, dear! Oh, dear! Oh, dear!" she cried, jumping out of Baby Bear's bed. She ran out of the bedroom, down the stairs, out of the front door and all the way back home – and she never ever came back to the forest again!